Daddy's Sandwich

This Faber book belongs to

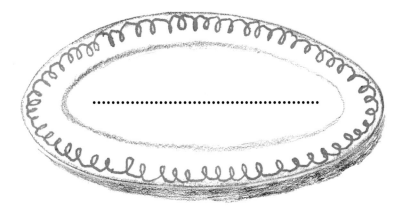

....

'I did like it a lot, it is very funny.'
Keira, age 3

'Let's read it again! Let's read it again!
Let's read it again!'
Alex, age 3

'Thank you to the lady who wrote it and
whoever did the pictures. Now I am off to
make a sandwich for my daddy. Mummy
can you help me with the toaster?'
Daisy, age 5 and mum Joanna

'That book is CRAZY! That sandwich
would taste disgusting! It was fun.'
Izzy, age 5

'She's so silly my face fell off.'
Dexter, age 3

'It was very funny. It made me think
of what I would put into MY Daddy's
sandwich and that was even funnier.'
Ibrahim, age 4

'I will make daddy a sandwich but I won't
be in it as his cheese is tooooooo stinky.'
Joseph, age 3

'That was good. That's a big sandwich.
Why didn't she put jam in it?'
Finley, age 4

'I like the kitty cat.'
Ellis, age 3

For darling Ruby,
the most quirky and
creative of little chefs X
P. J.

For my dad
L. H.

First published in the UK in 2015
This edition first published in the USA in 2017
by Faber and Faber Limited
Bloomsbury House,
74–77 Great Russell Street, London WC1B 3DA

Text copyright © Pip Jones, 2015
Illustration copyright © Laura Hughes, 2015
Design by Ness Wood

HB ISBN 978–0–571–31182–8
PB ISBN 978–0–571–31183–5

10 9 8 7 6 5

The moral rights of Pip Jones and Laura Hughes have been asserted.
A CIP record for this book is available from the British Library.

↠ A FABER PICTURE BOOK ↞

Daddy's Sandwich

Written by
Pip Jones

Illustrated by
Laura Hughes

ff

FABER & FABER

'Daddy, would you like a sandwich, with all your favourite things?'

'Mmm!
Yes please.'

Now, what does Daddy **really** like?

bread

Daddy loves white bread, crusty on the outside.

Daddy loves butter,

but not **too** much.

Daddy loves cheese that's a **teeny** bit stinky.

Daddy loves tomato,

with the green
bit pulled off.

Daddy loves biscuits
dunked in tea.

Daddy loves
his slippers,
'cos they're old
and **very** cosy.

Daddy loves his newspaper, but **not** when it's been crinkled.

Daddy loves his phone, with the sound up **very** loud.

Daddy loves the TV, and all those **boring** sports shows.

Daddy loves his bike, but it's **far** too **big** . . .

Oh! These will do!

Daddy loves Mum's bubble bath,
he sits in there for ages.

Daddy loves his camera, and I'm **not** supposed to touch it . . . **but** maybe just this once.

Daddy loves his banjo.

And his toolbelt.

And his deckchair.

Daddy loves . . .

my jelly beans.

Hmm . . .

And my jigsaws!

My drawings!

My paddling pool!

My pop-up
books!

Daddy's sandwich
is nearly finished!

Just a **great big squirt**
of ketchup, and a slice of bread
to go on top.

But I think there's
something missing . . .

I know!

More than
anything,
Daddy
loves . . .

'DADDY! Your sandwich is ready!'